P9-DIZ-651

To:
From:
Date:

A That Sounds Fun Book for Kids

WHAT SOUNDS FUN TO YOU?

New York Times bestselling author

ANNIE F. DOWNS

Illustrated by Jennie Poh

Revell
a division of Baker Publishing Group
Grand Rapids, Michigan

Published by Revell
a division of Baker Publishing Group
PO Box 6287, Grand Rapids, MI 49516-6287
www.revellbooks.com

Printed in Canada

Library of Congress Cataloging-in-Publication Data
Names: Downs, Annie F., 1980– author.
Title: What sounds fun to you? / Annie F. Downs.
Description: Grand Rapids, Michigan : Revell, a division of Baker Publishing Group, [2021] | Series: A that sounds fun book for kids | Audience: Ages 6–8 | Audience: Grades 2–3
Identifiers: LCCN 2021003818 | ISBN 9780800738754 (cloth) | ISBN 9781493426782 (ebook)
Subjects: LCSH: Children—Recreation—Juvenile literature. | Play—Juvenile literature. | Outdoor recreation for children—Juvenile literature. | Creative activities and seat work—Juvenile literature.
Classification: LCC GV182.9 .D696 2021 | DDC 790.1/922—dc23
LC record available at https://lccn.loc.gov/2021003818

The proprietor is represented by Alive Literary Agency, www.aliveliterary.com.

Typesetting by William Overbeeke

21 22 23 24 25 26 27 7 6 5 4 3 2 1

You are some
of the best people I know.
I'm so thankful
for the fun
you bring to my life.

Hi, friend. I'm Annie.

And this book is
all about
fun.

And there are lots of ways to find fun on this big, beautiful earth—like in our neighborhood and around the places that we live.

You can ride bikes with a friend
or cartwheel round and round.

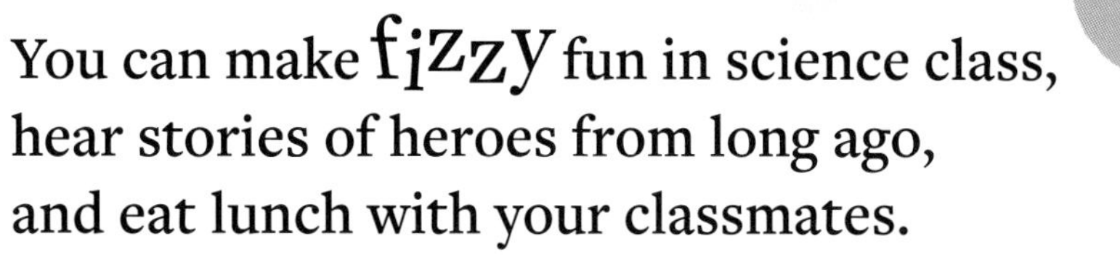

You can make fizzy fun in science class,
hear stories of heroes from long ago,
and eat lunch with your classmates.

From the playground to the classroom,
fun is around every corner.

When school is done, you can hug a furry friend. And your little brother knows just what game to play together!

Rainy days don’t have to soak all our fun!

Jump in puddles.

Race paper boats through tiny streams.

Or stay home and bake cookies.
That sounds like a delicious solution.

There's something really special about the farmers market.

You can find a ripe red tomato, meet the man who makes goat cheese, and get a treat on the way out—
ice cream, please!

I'm looking for
my friend Sammy.
He's got a blue hat on.
Can you help me find him?

CAN WE GO PLAY AT THE PARK?

Swings go so high, and kites go higher! Playing soccer, going down the slide, chasing leaves.

It is ALL fun!

Helping out in the kitchen is fun for everyone—
snapping green beans, swish-swashing the dishes clean,
and banging the washed pots as you put them away.

Going on a walk with Grandma
is the best kind of fun—
she sees all the birds
and knows their names.
And she always shares
her minty green bubblegum.

My friend Kendra lost her red glove—do you see it? Can you help her find it?

When it's cold outside, bundle up just right
and make a snow angel on the ground.

Sledding and skating with your neighbors

or catching a few snowflakes
on your tongue is super fun—
and then run back inside for hot cocoa!

The place where you worship
God can be fun.

Sing a loud song.

Whisper a small prayer.

And hug your best friend!

Building castles in the sand
and jumping in the waves
before a picnic lunch with crunchy
chips is always fun. Then it's time
to chase a seagull down the beach.

Don't you have
the most fun lying
in the soft grass
and looking up

at the funny clouds

and laughing together with your friends

while the wind blows?

Splish, splash!

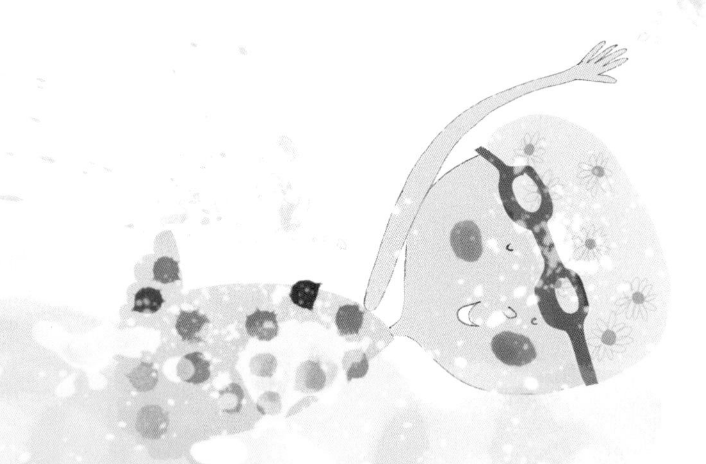

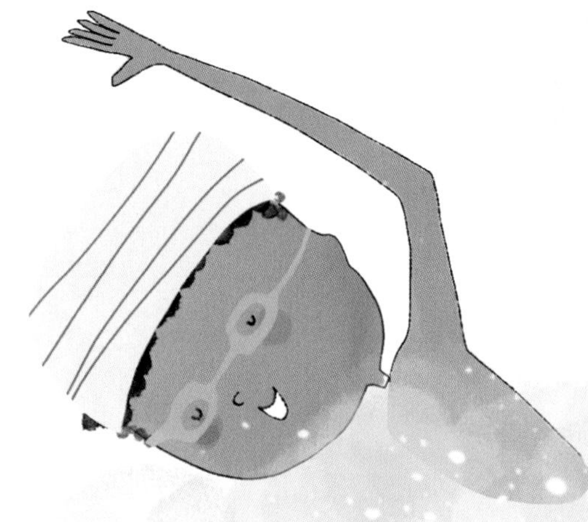

You can have lots of fun at the swimming pool!

Races and sliding, card games and diving.

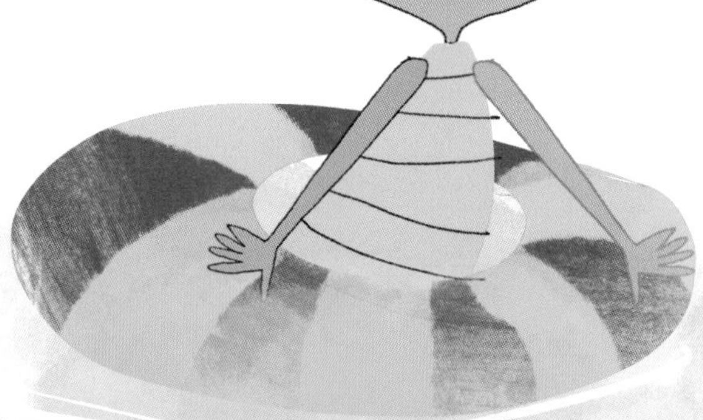

Puffy piles of cotton candy. Petting zoos.
Roller coasters and big balloons.

Different people love different things,
but we all have fun at the fair!

Pretend you are a pirate
out on the wild seas.
Or a clown in a three-ring show!

What good times can you have
with what's in your mind?

There is always SOMETHING to do
when there is NOTHING to do.
Build a blanket fort.
Fold an origami bird.
Read a book
for fun!

When carrots need picking and sunflowers need watering, when trees need climbing and flowers need sniffing, the garden is the best place to find fun.

Bunnies love the garden! How many rabbits do you see looking for carrots?

Do you like to paint a picture?
Do you like to tell a story?

Or lie in a hammock with a daydream?
We can all like different fun things
and still be great pals.

You don't have to be famous
to make music. Put a bunch of dry beans
in a jar, seal it, and shake it.
That SOUNDS fun!

A slow turtle is easy to find.

A fast gerbil is fun to watch.

A pet is a friend who loves
to hang out all the time!

Watch for a shooting star or play chess with your mom.
When the world gets quiet, fun can be quiet too.

If nighttime
makes you feel afraid,
look for something fun to do!

Everywhere you go, if you look around, people are having fun.

So go out and do something that sounds fun to you, and I will do the same!

But before you go, I want to know—

what
sounds
fun
to YOU?

And here's some more fun for you! Can you find these things inside the book?